In the **Country,**
In the **City**

Fay Robinson • Photographs by Brent Jones and Malcolm Cross

Rigby

Children live in the country.

Children live in the city.

Children play in the country.

Children play in the city.

Children run in the country.

Children run in the city.

Children swing in the country.